Sea, Salt, and Air

by Miriam Bat-Ami

illustrated by Mary O'Keefe Young

MACMILLAN PUBLISHING COMPANY   NEW YORK

MAXWELL MACMILLAN CANADA   TORONTO

MAXWELL MACMILLAN INTERNATIONAL

NEW YORK   OXFORD   SINGAPORE   SYDNEY

In memory of my grandparents and my father,
and for my mother to share with her grandchildren —M. B.-A.

To Myles and Pamela —M. O'K. Y.

Every summer there comes a time
when Mom sits out on the porch rocker saying,
"I bet it's hot enough you could fry an egg on the sidewalk,"
and I can't stay out past dusk
because of all the gnats working their jaws
or whatever they work when they fly around,
hungry.
"It's time we took the kids to the beach," she says.
"They're shooting up like weeds.
Grandparents need to see all that."

And every year my sister and my brother and I just can't wait.
The day before packing day we all troop up to the attic,
rummaging
through two-piece suits that are missing one piece,
through men's blue bathing suits that Dad and Grandpa wear
so their knees look like knobby table legs,
through sneakers that still leak a stream of sand
when you turn them upside down.

My sister holds up two old swim caps,
the kind that look like plastic leaves
sprouted on your wet skull,
blue and pink and white leaves
you can pull and snap.
"There she is, Miss America."
We sing, shaking our funny-colored heads.
And the leaves dance with us.

Then, all of a sudden,
our feet and our hands want to dance like the leaves.
"Beach fever," we whisper.
It's a fever that comes long before we load the car
and stays until we're home again.
So we try to settle down, working quietly
like ants or bees.
Outside the sky turns from red to dark blue
while the sand sifts through my toes.
And the tops of our heads are hot.

And I don't know who starts it.
We all lift our arms up
and swing them down again, faster and faster,
making loud whooshing sounds,
Whoo…sheh! Whoo…oo…SHEH!
We grow higher and higher,
rushing against the shore, pounding,
devouring the sand in   great   big   gulps.
We fling ourselves into each other,
wildly laughing.

Then, just before we go bumping down the attic stairs with our suitcases,
there's this thing that comes over us.
My sister stares at a faded shell.
My brother blows into Dad's old snorkel,
and I play with a flip-flop I used to wear
when I was real real little.

We sit, looking through old photos we all laugh at:
Mom in a teensy-weensy bikini—she's lying on a rock and waving;
Dad in his navy uniform—he's wearing funny owlish glasses;
a little girl squeezed inside a huge square snowball snowsuit.
"It was cold in Poland," Grandma likes to say, chuckling.
I close my eyes, looking deep and long and wide.
I wonder about all those things that happened long before we were ever born.
I wonder about things that haven't happened yet.

And every year, on the day before we leave, we do everything fast.
We even eat fast.
The next morning when we stumble out of bed, it's still black outside,
so we feel our way to the car
and load up for the great adventure:

hard candies, apples, oranges, suntan lotion, maps, toilet paper, drinks, paper,
crayons, a deck of cards, sunglasses, red and black licorice, barbecue potato chips,
peanut butter and jelly sandwiches.
We squeeze balloon-shaped suitcases into the trunk
first in one way and then in another
until even the side holes are crammed with things.

Dad slams the trunk down twice.
We're off, bumping down the road.

And the day always passes with games like ghost and hangman,
or calling out license plates from different states,
and guessing how much tolls will cost.
We stop at a diner for lunch.
"Make sure they all go to the bathroom," Dad says to Mom.
Still, one of us has to go pee just after we've started up again.

Sometime before dark, my sister and brother and I fight for the front seat,
away from the mess we've all made.
Dad curses softly because he's lost.
"Why don't you stop and ask!" says Mom.
"Why don't you take over!" yells Dad.

Then we play our favorite nighttime game.
"PIDIDDLE!" We shout,
depending on who's the first one
to spot a car with only one headlight on.
My brother pretends he's going to kiss one of us.
My sister and I scream until we're all hitting each other.
"It's her fault!" "It's his fault!"
"MOM, MAKE THEM STOP!"

"STOP IT RIGHT NOW OR WE'RE TURNING AROUND!" snaps Mom.

Getting close to Nantasket, we can taste salt on our lips.
Mom tells us family stories, ones we hear every summer:
how Grandma's beach house almost fell down one high-tide year,
how Grandpa nearly lost his wool business,
how Mom cut a nickel out of the ice one hard winter....
Mom's voice sounds full of foam and bubbles.
I can smell salt in her hair.
And she seems changed somehow,
not like our mother...like somebody else's child.
And the stories rush in and out through our open mouths
like the sea,
and the salt,
and the air.

Every year, Grandma's on the porch, waiting.
We fall out of the cramped car
like a huge pile of clothes tumbling out of a hot dryer.
Grandpa shepherds us into the kitchen where we nearly fall asleep
over bowls of strange soup, cold and beet-red,
that we eat only at Grandma's.
And all week long we live in that nowhere beach time
somewhere between grandparent time and our time.

Early in the mornings, my brother, my sister, and I
run down to the beach.
Grandpa's white sandals flap behind us.
When we reach the water's edge, we stop, waiting,
while Grandpa walks slowly
a little past his knees
into the water.

"*Chah, Chah,*" he says.
Bending, he splashes water under his armpits
and onto his chest that's white and hairy.
Then he crosses his arms, slapping his shoulders.
"*Chah, Chah.* Not so cold," he laughs, daring us.
So we rush in.
The water freezes our toes.
Small and pimply goose bumps grow on our arms.
But then we get used to it.

All morning long we ride the waves.
Our eyes sting.
Our noses feel dry and wrinkled, peeling.
Our underwater bodies stretch out longer and longer.
We are whales, and porpoises, and many-legged octopi,
plunging into the green, salty water.

When the sun sits squashed like a pancake inside the sky,
we dash out of the water and hop over the hot sand.
Grandma and Mom wave to us, their arms full.
And we eat cheese and sand
and lettuce and sand
and bread and sand.
Then we buy push-ups or pops that make our tongues blue,
and our freezing lips purple.

Afternoons, we bury each other in sand.
"Mummy, be still!" one of us commands.
I feel what it's like wanting to lift my arms to my mouth or eyes,
unable to touch my face with my hands.
Or we play in the little pools left by the high tide.
We try to stand like statues
while the wet sand pulls against our ankles,
and our feet sink into growing holes.

At the end of the day, we walk along the beach.
We find open clamshells.
Silently, we bend our heads,
peering into the shiny space where a clam once lived.
And we feel as if we're staring into secret places
we're not supposed to see.

On the grass behind Grandma and Grandpa's house
we hose off our feet and shower in the basement
where the boards smell like old seaweed.

Nights, we all sit out on the front porch.
Our eyes want to close, and our voices are foghorns,
calling out to each other.
Then Dad tells us stories:
about his Mom selling insurance on the phone,
pretending she was many people;
about Charlie, his pet myna bird, who ate grapes and spaghetti;
about the imaginary animals living in the closet
outside his bedroom—fierce animals
who might come out when his parents were asleep.
There are some stories Dad tells us every year.
But there are things he says only once, and I'll always remember.

At the end of last summer, Dad took us down to the beach
where it was quiet all by itself.
He told us how he saw his Mom in every one of us, somewhere.
He told us how his mother died, and how his Dad died.
His Dad never knew him, but he tries to know us.
My sister and my brother and I touched our Dad
like you touch something you think is going to disappear or break.
And I wanted to tell him what I'd wanted to say all summer long:
how I wouldn't wear sunsuits anymore because sunsuits are for babies.
And all summer long all those things we did every year were different, somehow.
They made me want to cry, even though I wasn't really sad.
Sometimes I'd want a bikini real badly,
and sometimes I just wanted to go to the penny candy store
that has a low roof so you have to bend down.
Then I thought about how it was when I didn't have to bend down,
and I wanted to cry. I wanted to tell him how, all summer long,
I wanted to go home, and I wanted to *never* go home:

I thought if I did go home, I'd find out I *was* different.
But the words stayed stuck in my throat, even when I coughed.

And then, before I even knew it, I blurted out,
"Do you think I'll ever be beautiful?"

Dad touched my cheek softly like *I* was going to disappear.
And I knew I didn't have to tell him all those things I felt.
He just knew.

Then it was packing day again, like it always is.
And the same and the different mixed together, like it always does now.
Mom looks at Grandma and Grandpa in a quiet, sad kind of way.
Our stomachs hurt, even without aching.
We feel cold and tired like beach fever came and went.
We kiss Grandma and Grandpa.
I can smell Grandma's face cream.
I can taste the salt on Grandpa's cheek.
"Grandpa," I say, quickly and quietly so only he hears,
"Next year I'm going to stay underwater for the longest time.
I'm going to buy a surfboard so I can ride on top of the waves.
Next year I'm going to have a fluorescent bikini so you can see me
coming down the beach even when it's dark.
Next year I'm going to...I'm going to do all these new things
I don't even know about yet
so you'll have to wait and see.
You'll have to keep your camera ready."
I kiss Grandma and Grandpa in a new and special way that makes my lips hurt.

Then we all wave, riding down the block,
watching them stand
like statues
trying to be
perfectly still.

Library of Congress Cataloging-in-Publication Data. Bat-Ami, Miriam. Sea, salt, and air / by Miriam Bat-Ami ; illustrated by Mary O'Keefe Young. — 1st ed. p. cm. Summary: Every summer the family stays with Grandma and Grandpa at the beach, and every summer they do the same things, but this summer the narrator struggles with growing up. ISBN 0-02-708495-7 [1. Beaches—Fiction. 2. Growth—Fiction. 3. Grandparents—Fiction. 4. Family life—Fiction.] I. Young, Mary O'Keefe, ill. II. Title. PZ7.B2939Se 1993 [Fic]—dc20 91-34140